Cage of Wild Cries

Cage of Wild Cries

Claudia Menza

MOSAIC PRESS
Oakville·New York·London

CANADIAN CATALOGUING IN PUBLICATION DATA

Menza, Claudia, 1947 -
        Cage of wild cries

Poems.
ISBN 0-88962-446-1 (bound) ISBN 0-88962-445-3 (pbk.)

I. Title.

PS3563.E69C33 1990   811'.54   C90-094662-8

Published by MOSAIC PRESS, P.O. Box 1032, Oakville, Ontario, L6J 5E9, Canada. Offices and warehouse at 1252 Speers Road, Units # 1&2, Oakville, Ontario, L6L 5N9, Canada.

Mosaic Press acknowledges the assistance of the Canadian Council and the Ontario Arts Council in support of its publishing programme.

Copyright © Claudia Menza, 1990
Cover Illustration by Henri Rousseau
Design by Marion Black
Typeset by Jackie Ernst
Printed and bound in Canada.

ISBN 0-88962-445-3 PAPER   ISBN 0-88962-446-1 CLOTH

MOSAIC PRESS:
in Canada:
        MOSAIC PRESS, 1252 Speers Road, Units # 1&2, Oakville, Ontario, L6L 5N9, P.O. Box 1032, Oakville, Ontario, L6J 5E9, Canada.

In the United States:
        Riverrun Press Inc., 1170 Broadway, Suite 807, New York, NY 10001, U.S.A.

In the U.K.:
        John Calder (Publishers) Ltd., 9-15 Neal Street, London, WC2 H9TU, England.

to D. H. Melhem
poet, mentor, friend

ACKNOWLEDGMENTS

Some of these poems have appeared in the following publications:

The Dream Book: An Anthology of Writings by Italian American Women (New York: Schocken Books), *Confrontation, Dasein, Light, Ploughshares, Softball, The Spoken Wheel,* and *The Villager.*

And with thanks to...my friends, who have listened year after year...my parents, for the rich education they have provided me...my sister, for her constant confirmation...my husband, for his relentless encouragement of my work...and my publisher, without whom, quite obviously, this book would not exist.

A NOTE

What interests me about life is the "B" side of the record, the flip side that is not and was never meant to be the hit. When something is not meant to make a splash, it has the luxury of some very interesting movements in the water. It will tell you as much about the nature of swimming as the Olympics. If I see a verbal battle between two dog owners, I'm much more likely to observe the behavior of the dogs than the masters. If I'm looking at a painting of a garden done in dreamy pastels, I'll probably notice the small dot of red the painter has used on a blade of grass somewhere in the background. The small things give another way of looking at the world--like entering a house from the back door--and often bring an unexpected joke with them: I remember seeing a western in which one cowpoke was consulting his Timex in a picture that takes place in 1883!

. . . .

I let the image do the work of my mind and heart. For me, the image is the idea, the feeling, at its most visceral, its most tangible. It is the workhorse of the imagination, that which provides the metaphor, a sort of translation of the senses, the materialization of that which normally appears as a viscous white substance hanging about our ankles.

. . . .

People have sometimes asked me why I don't write a novel; the assumption is that if you can write one form you can write another. This is not necessarily true. And, in fact, I don't hear the world as a novel, much as I love to read them. I *hear* poetry. I hear the world in beats and phrases, in rhythms and images, not sentences. And I know the end of the poem as soon as I begin it. In a novel each sentence moves you toward some end which neither the reader nor, indeed, the novelist knows until it is there. The vision of a novel becomes clear only when that journey of sentences has been taken. But in a poem, the beginning contains the end (and vice versa) so that the vision is instantaneous. A poem is a bit like getting hit on the head by an apple falling from the tree: your head begins to hurt immediately.

. . . .

The section "Cage of Wild Cries" was written during the final year of Franco's reign in Spain. The poems are terse, self-contained, reflecting the character of the people under that dictatorship. They mirror color and passion and sometimes violence, but under control. Hence, a cage of wild cries.

7

The "Brave City" poems are about my native country, New York City, the battles we wage daily against the forces that would do us in. The Bronx Zoo poem I think of as a metaphor for New York: like a zoo, New York is subject to the terrible irony of preserving lives and cultures and ideas that might not otherwise survive, but at the same time it is a cage in which these are trapped.

About the love poems, what can I say? They are love poems.

Dogs are a very important part of my life. To me, they are the sweetest, gentlest creatures on this earth because they do not judge. They don't care how much money you make or what language you speak or what you look like. They care only that your heart is right--and they can smell it. Therefore, any reading I give, any book of my work, must contain at least one dog poem. This is my willing and happy sacrifice to the Dog God.

"Anima/Animus" is all about ironies, the other side of the coin flipped up for observation, where tails are really the tale.

. . . .

Why the cage, and the cries? Because a poem is the device in which the poet expresses what is longing, bursting, to get out. But the bigger metaphor is for all of us: the horse in "Some Proud Head" whose life is bridled, the cabbages in "The Vegetable Garden at Kent Cliffs, New York" who long to be duchesses, the creatures in "Monsters" who are so desperate for love. It is you, and me, rattling the bones of our cages, trying desperately to speak what sometimes cannot be spoken.

Claudia Menza
New York, June, 1989

CONTENTS

CAGE OF WILD CRIES

BRAVE CITY

LOVE'S POEMS

CAGE OF WILD CRIES

I began "Cage of Wild Cries" in July, 1974, in the town of Fuen-
girola, on the southern coast of Spain. The beaches were bright with
people; cool, tranquil atriums enclosed intimate gardens; tiles of
magenta and blue, red and yellow, patterned a park bench or a flight
of steps; cathedral altars were studded with gold and jewels; bullrings
flew vivid banners. And yet I sensed uneasiness, uncertainty. Gener-
alissimo Francisco Franco was dying. No one asked questions. It was
like a sunshower, the air struck with rain, the sun shining. The very
landscape, like the faces of the people, was gentle but tense, at once
lush and barren: hibiscus bloomed in a scarlet rage at the edge of a
desert; beggars persisted in the shadow of the Alhambra--everywhere
beauty and pageantry at odds with the events of history, like the lure
of a cactus flower, whose petals will draw blood.

The Restaurant with Birds, Fuengirola

To get there,
you go back,
through old streets,
far from the pack of hotels
tearing at a strip of beach.

In the restaurant with birds,
sunlight slants through
pale bamboo, the only roof,
to an openwork cage of generous proportion:
great gaudy macaws and parrots of a raucous green
puff up their feathers with thick, hooked beaks;
a yellow-ochre toucan throws back its head
and cracks the air with wild cries.

Málaga Harbor

Usually in this place
you can hear the cries of travelers,
luggage loaded and unloaded,
ropes squeaking against the wharf.

Today
the crowd loosely assembled on the dock
sets sight
on a ship like a fine white fleck
winking
toward the harbor.

A blue tug idling in port waits too:
bow to stern, a small, rough dog struts,
casting hard looks at the horizon
while the breeze blows back his ears.

Balloons escape,
and scarves excited by the wind
splash the air.

At the edge of the dock
children slip down
the little stone steps
to dip their feet.

The Dog on the Sidewalk at Málaga

In the middle of the sidewalk, dozing,
a raggedy Málaga dog soaks up the noonday sun,
enjoying the heat on his belly.
His scrawny legs,
fully extended, undisturbed,
force pedestrians to one side:
shoes, the wheels of grocery carts,
the tips of walking sticks funnel
into a narrow lane at his back.
Waking slowly,
he stretches against the warm, rough tiles,
rolls to his back,
pushes up the sky with his legs, and,
like a switch thrown,
shifts to his other side,
changing the course of noonday Málaga
to the place his legs once were.

At the Alcázar Palace, Seville

A tapestry at the Alcázar Palace
depicts a hunting scene in which
the pursuing riders scatter in the clearing
to scan the adjacent woods,
horses every which way,
while, sprawled in the foreground,
sleek, wine-colored dogs
lounge in easy groups
played out in the grass.

In the performance of small things,
dogs are unsurpassed:
they'll bark to Music,
sit for Company.
At crucial moments,
they become perverse:
walk off,
won't budge,
their masters mere abstractions
in the distance.

The Mosque at Córdoba

We enter the forest:
the opening through which we slipped
from the clearing
closes behind us
like reverse birth.
Skylights filter the dusty light
through arcades--
stone branches grown
one into the other.

Worshippers who deserted the site
pulled carpets from the floor,
left branches
stripped of banners,
returning them
to marble primeval.

Confronting the maze,
we wander among trunks
like children tucked away in time,
our paths of breadcrumbs
eaten by birds.

The disturbance of any twig
brings thunder to the branches;
we dare not call
lest our voices
roar toward heaven.

The Beach at Fuengirola

Under striped canopies
bathers rest,
catching the sun in their suits.

Beached at the water's edge,
two old women
raise their black skirts to the sea.

Holding their hems
as they wade to the knee,
they scoop up the retreating tide,
splash water into their open blouses.

Mijas

I.

Ah, Mijas!
Out of the olive scrub of mountains
you suddenly come into view,
a cluster of houses white-washed to a clean
bright cleft bedded down high above the valley.
The sun cuts you like a jewel,
and from every angle you throw sparks
down the mountainside.

II.

I watch Mijas at mid-morning
from a shaded table at the *café*:
the men have come up from olive groves
on the backs of donkeys to drink
something cool at the *cantina*--a *cerveza,*
maybe *sangría,* a bit of sweet wine;
the donkeys wait beneath the pine trees,
their soft gray heads and flanks all
bright red tassels and bells.
A merchant hanging yellow and blue dresses
on the façade of his shop
passes the time of day with a farmer
whose goats nibble *sombreros* for sale.

III.

Two dogs sleeping outside the Casa Pepe
suddenly break for the street,
race past the *café,*
and drop out of sight,
leaving a light dust at the edge of town.

From where I sit
I can see the square--
the water pump ringed by geraniums
almost crimson in color.
Women drawing water there
engage each other in conversation.
Their voices filtering through the sunlight
tell me
there is no time in Mijas.

19

Two Granada Courtyards

I've seen the gardens of the Alhambra--
the way the Moorish sun breaks
upon a courtyard lush with roses;
how a long, shallow pool will lie down
beside the slender columns of a marble arcade.

Not much
like this courtyard,
a dank gap
of broken stones
where a beggar leans her head
against a sunless wall.
She grabs my arm as I pass,
and her pretty face,
pinched to a cameo,
touches me more than the courts of Moorish kings.

She wants money:
I give her
coins.

At the Hotel Murillo, Seville

Over the narrow street
our balconies touch.

My casement doors lie open,
facing yours, open too,
the curtain still drawn.

In the street beneath us
a wheelbarrow scrapes and bumps the cobblestones,
voices pass, and we are borne
on the backs of those voices,
down the length of the street
echoes carry us.

I see your feet
below the pale hem of the curtain:
shoes move under your breakfast table.

At the end of the street
the wheelbarrow clatters and shakes,
returning, louder now,
without its load.

Entering Tarifa

Noon in Tarifa:

the big hot sun is fixed
like a floodlight.
Its well-aimed rays expose
a town burnt,
not basking.

Low stucco houses bleach
in its fluorescent glare,
cracked by constant surveillance.
The white-robed inhabitants,
heads and faces wrapped like mummies,
twist away from a blinding light
in the public square:

there are no
trees to cast shadows.
A few thin palms
clatter and snap like whips,
shredded by a dry wind that cuts
to the heart of the city,
firing a volley of sharp, hot sand.

The Virgin Mary, Fuengirola

Mannequin Mother
wears white satin,
lace collar and cuffs.

Chalk cheeks
rouged to a fever;
blood lips.
The eyes
love struck by terror;
the palms upward.

An old woman in black
on the steps of the church
frowns as we pass. Or does she squint at
the sun coming down on the square?

In her thin lap
a small, dry hand
lies slightly open,
palm upward.

The Bullring at Ronda

Late afternoon:
sunlight casts the ring in gold dust
and drapes the stands in a saffron cloak.
Row upon row
benches of cool, smooth stone
shelter in a cloister of colonnades,
a Doric merry-go-round, mountain-embraced,
deserted with the coming dusk.
Silent, an ancient carousel rests,
pillowed in pines,
high in the Sierra Ronda.

I turn full circle at center arena.
Again the amphitheater flies ghostly banners
fading in at the edge of the dusk.
Spectators move forward in their seats, beckoned,
like the bull, by the twist of the cloak.

The empty bullring
shows no sign of blood.
But what the sun cannot bleach
remains: gore marks in a wooden wall,
scars of the years,
just below the stands.

In Doña Elvira Square, Seville

Evenings in Seville,
we'd sit beneath the heavy scent of the orange trees,
listening to a flamenco guitarist pluck roses.
He'd begin with the fingers of his right hand held
tightly against the strings like a closed flower;
then, one by one, he'd lay them back
like the petals of roses in bloom.

A slow, sinuous melody would rise,
at its climax dividing in two:
a brace of melodies curving out
over the square in semi-circular counterpoint,
a motif of roses espaliered against the evening,
and repeated in the tiles
of a nearby courtyard.

The Pall of Columbus, the Cathedral at Seville

In stride
the robes of his pall bearers
fly stiffly back.
Muscles cloaked in folds of sleeve
fight nearly unbearable weight.
For although these men are made of bronze
so is the pall which they carry.
Chins cast with the light of gods upon them,
they march as one into space,
the right feet of the first two carriers poised mid-air
as they step off the platform.

Agonies of angels
summoned to the site
offer holy water,
their fingers all but crushed by
the most delicate
scallop shells.

Columbus's ashes rest easy.
Let others bear the happenstance of history.

Leaving Tarifa

We have come to the end of the Western world.
In the distance
Gibraltar--Africa--
rises like the beacon toward which
we must sail.
We can expect no help with this voyage:
the sky is emitting the white light of storms
and the wind ties our ankles
with invisible cords.

Our hats go, blown like kisses
to whitecaps.
At the last minute
we remove our sunglasses
lest we lose those too.

The car, parked at the edge of the cliff,
is being rocked back and forth, teased by the wind which keeps easing
it over the precipice
without dropping it
into the sea.
We grip the fenders for support.
Our faces are singing at knifepoint
from sand flung up.

We believe we come without malice or prejudice,
but the wind has picked up
dread at the bone: a sudden gust sends our jackets
thumping against our chests and
fear howling in our ears.

We feel our way along the body of the car
like pall bearers.
Inside, we pull the doors shut
and move away from the windows.
The engine starts, for now.

BRAVE CITY

Bronx Zoo

I.

All extinct - -
or vanishing - -

The European Wild Horse
Steller's Sea Cow
Atlas Bear
Rodriguez Little Owl
Mysterious Macaw
Japanese Wolf
Indian Cheetah
the Flightless Night Heron

those long slipped away
abandoned to shallow graves.
Miniature markers
for small lives.
If we didn't kill them
we let them die
then stripped the jungle for coats and teeth

II.

In 1972 at the Bronx Zoo
30 foals were born to
the Mongolian Wild Horse,
one-quarter its entire population.
Of those 30, 17 survived
and that was the end
until this morning
when a single foal was born
just hours before the zoo opened
and now it's wobbling in the sun
barely able to stand the pressure
of its mother's tongue
as she licks its wet, bay coat

III.

It's molting season
and the bison
await their changes
like a herd of quiet, old men.
Their top coats have come all to pieces
but there are more underneath: many skins
pulled close to their broad, humped backs.
When the outer one frays
the next can weather winter

IV.

Lone Wolf
in the Wolf Wood
separated from prairies
from unbounded forests
where the others run hunting
hearts pulled to packs

Utterly stilled
head dropped
no place to go
that doesn't meet with fence

V.

Emus are so big
they don't have to fly.
In 1932 in western Australia
they were attacked for trampling fences,
pursued first by a machine gun unit
and later by bounty hunters
but it was no use:
the emus scattered
then turned and stayed put,
deflecting bullets.
Home is where the heart is:
look how the slope of their feathers
recalls thatched roofs.
Nothing scares emus.

VI.

Hooded Vultures
feathered like judges
the Père David Deer
the yellow-eyed
Greater Sand Hill Crane
Barbary Apes
the Crepuscular Crooner
candy corn-beaked Parrots and Silver Gulls
flights of Pelicans
trailing their great webbed feet
like clothes caught
in the lip of a suitcase

VII.

Jaguar dreaming in the afternoon
paws quivering against the stone

Jaguar shaking in a drying bed
ears twitching in a tawny sleep

floors murmur
but you cannot speak

dream, Jaguar, dream

Pocket Park, Little Italy

I.

So. It's come down to this:
pocket park, frail parody of
past estates. More what belongs
in a pocket: a handkerchief dropped
at the foot of predatory buildings,
abandoned to half-sun, nothing but
frayed trees and
peeling yellow benches.

Impossible park!
The corner of Sixth Ave. & Houston St.,
the rattling bones of idling engines,
and then the sudden scrape of gears against
a sky already rent with sound.

For one quiet spot!
A moment not uprooted
by the quake of dissonant cargo,
this painful rendition of
The New World Symphony.
If only the *aii-eee!* you hear
were a lark and not
the whine of air brakes:
trucks stampeding the Holland Tunnel.

But there they sit,
hands folded in their laps,
hugging the hem of the park,
which hangs behind them
like a rude scrim.
You can be their photographer
any day of the week--see them?
Staring straight into the camera.

II.

The old men play chess
at tables made for that purpose:
concrete mushrooms the park
has sprouted, painted with
black and white squares,
an industrial fresco where
rooks and knights wage
silent battle.
Short and stocky as pawns,
the players sit beneath the ragged trees,
their gnarled brown arms knotted
across their chests, trunks grown
one into the other.
The air is tight:
they are contemplating moves.
At their elbows, small wooden boxes
lie emptied of men.
Observers keep their hands
in their pockets while
positioning small stones
with their feet.

The old women sit close by,
bags lumpy with groceries
from which they pull for comparison
heads of broccoli and cauliflower,
brides their bouquets.
They--unlike the men, for whom language
is but dim memory--are never at a loss
for words. They pummel each other
with rapid-fire Italian,
rolling vowels off their tongues,
executing consonants with a definition
long gone from their bodies, and then
punctuating the air
like a sentence--*eh!*

The young women are alluring, and sour,
old enough to apply the pressure of
their beauty, but too young to have the power of
the old women, into whose conversation they enter
only the occasional word.
They don't have much
to say: groceries have not yet become
metaphor, nor their bones fit topic
for discussion. They concentrate on
retaining their shapes, and wear
light cotton dresses, and sandals
made in Italy.
They have just picked up their children from school
and occupy themselves with
pushing the girls' hair out of their eyes
and with pulling up the boys' zippers,
which always seem to be open.

III.

Now, he
is impeccably dressed for another century:
a suit the color of doves with a pin stripe,
glossy black shoes--one feels the presence of spats--
and a bowler set firmly
to his head.
A gold-braid watch chain hangs like
a garland across his vest.
On his face, which is tired
and dignified, he wears
a waxed handlebar moustache.
One hand he rests on his walking stick,
and the other on his knee, except when
he moves it to cover
her hand.

I have seen them
even in the rain,
when he opens
a large black umbrella
over her head.

She
wears bright green slacks of a stretchy
synthetic material, too tight and too short,
and a white cotton blouse with
an absurdly large collar, something
a clown would wear.
Someone other than she--other than a woman--
has dressed her: the slacks are pulled up to her chest
and the blouse twists away from her body
the way bedclothes flee your dreams
and you wake with something caught
around your neck.
She sits cross-legged on the bench,
a hand on each knee, rocking
back and forth, back and forth,
taking her bows,
a big foolish smile on her face.

IV.

He remembers parks from their past:

lush, cool cocoons,
how the trees would reach for each other
across paths so broad it seemed impossible to touch,
let alone embrace, printing
wild, tangled kisses
on the blushing brick.
The sweet let-run of deep, fresh lawns,
walks laid in patterns of
intersecting fret and herringbone.
And where there was no lake or river,
fountains provided that pleasure
an indispensable to the Villa d'Este
as it was to the atria of Pompeii:
the sound of water!
Nature and the nature of man
stretched out together
beneath the Italian sun.
Those were parks, eh?

No excuse of a rose,
no apology of grass.
The air was redolent, green,
and from the branches unseen birds sang
lunatic melodies, those yet compelling cries
one cannot understand.

And so too did they, this man and this woman,
speak a private language.
She wore crisp white cotton
and a wide-brimmed hat to keep off the sun,
although the trees were a hat already:
filtered beams fell to the path,
tracing her steps like footlights.
She was so girlish, so, so, so--his.

When she tired of strolling,
they sat upon a bench,
a wrought-iron wonder of curlicues and flourishes,
to watch other lovers tender small affections,
as if witnessing happiness
increased their own.
He held her hand, nurturing
a tender grape in new soil. She spoke
through her fingers, a language he understood
in the context of birds.
She wanted for nothing
with him.
Afternoon drifted toward evening
like dying leaves
down a country lane.
If he lacked for gaiety, well.
She watched sparrows poke the underbrush
like a squad of Keystone Cops.
And he watched her,
his pleasure her pleasure at
attending sparrows.
And what's wrong with that?
Pleasure is pleasure, she believed,
however it comes.

The Elevator Man

I.

between
the 3rd
& the 6th,
the elevator man
notices the book
I am reading

I am halfway
through
and having a hard
time of it

the elevator man
says,
great book,
read it
on my way up
yesterday

it's a long haul
from the basement,
he says

II.

several days later
the elevator man
picks me up
on the 3rd

I'm writing a novel,
he says

he presses 6,
I get out

you're in it
too,
he says

Why I Hate the Ballet
to Barbara Holland, whose work inspired this

She appears weightless, doll-like,
dressed in that ridiculous word: tutu.
She is a trophy for whom
he is seeking a pedestal,
he who is permitted to move
with his feet touching the ground.

She is to be arranged
like so much furniture,
first here, then there,
then here again,
as if her position were never quite
satisfactory.

And how complicitous, how willing she is
is this travesty of womanhood,
spreading her legs as he lifts,
her arms fluttering, the wings of
a desperate bird.
She points her toes, broken from
years of balancing on
such precarious tips,
then remembers her face, on which she screws
a relentless smile.

Just like that
she's displayed caught
in the act of flying.
He holds her up
till the cheering stops
then drops her to the floor
like an unfinished thought.

Now he can dance, knowing
she will wait face down
till he returns to drag her
from the wings, her resistance
coy, a mere plot twist.

He pulls her to her feet
and sets her spinning in place,
an orbit he defines
within the compass of his arms.
Weary is out of the question:
the orchestra is at her heels,
notes are storming her from the pit,
faster and faster she goes
until the music breathes its last
and she is a blur of sparkling dust.

He at least wears something with
the semblance of a shoe, the hint of a buckle,
while she is still in her slippers,
appropriate footwear for women
since Cinderella slipped her tired toes
into one of glass.
Ah fantasy! the perfect fit.
One turn on the dance floor
and the prince insists
he loves her for herself.

finally flowers

finally flowers
have come to our street

the winter which
pursued us with
Arctic cold
and a wind that howled
in canyons formed
by heightening snowdrifts
(we hooked dogs to our sleds)
(we skied to the supermarket)
now gives us
an ironic spring:

no awakening crocus
nor field of daffodils
to match the nature
of our winter

but flowers
stuck in a garbage can
outside the door of
the Seventh Day Adventist Church
their colors in fade
retaining still a whisp-
er of formal arrangement

and here and there
a tentative head droops
like daisies on the hat of a young girl
slightly askew in spring

bouquet:
tender a ruined fragrance--
we'll take you as you are

touch us with spring

Some Proud Head

I.

Some proud head that is.
I don't call pulled back
proud.
A policeman's grip upon
a horse's reins is not
head held high.

This is noble?
The tension of a strap
against the neck?
The cut of the bit
inside the mouth?
This is stately, these blinders
closing like night
about the eyes?

A breeze would do as well, the tug of
morning at his mane. Watch him willingly lift
his head, ears to catch
the singing wind.

II.

At the jab of his knees, I move forward.
A tug of the reins is hold back.
Trust is my rider who keeps our flanks
from the traffic's jaws. Traffic is a roaring column of light
before my blinded eyes.
Hope is a field where a rainbow has come down.
What little grass reaches these dumb hooves
grows between the cobblestones.
Trees are something a park has.

The pull of the bit is stop.
Metal is not something you eat.
Metal is for flying in, driving in.
Metal is for killing with.
The sweet soak of oats inside my mouth
is what I like. The crunch of an apple
in my teeth.

A saddle keeps my rider straight.
I forget what it's like to gallop without one.
A burden is something upon your back.
Only at night, within my stall, am I unbound.
The stars are outside. I never see them.
While voices fall like dying leaves,
and cars sleep in the fold of the curb,
I can hear them hanging the moon.

Morning is work-time: saddles and straps
and bits and blinders.
I suppose my rider is a kindly man, but metal is metal,
and leather, the hide of my compatriots, cuts too.
Hope is a rainbow that comes down in a field.
Proud is what I am
despite the strap of morning.

Street Orange

Day turns metal.
The sky slips
through fissures in the street,
through cracks in the waking
world.

At Sheridan Square
a streetsweeper abandons its route
and begins advancing on West 4th
like a stray tank.

As it pulls garbage
into a blackened mouth,
an orange escapes
its brushy teeth
and rolls back to the curb.

I'm staying, it says,
opening its rind
to the gutter.

Out of all that dirt
a bright-orange orange.

At the Opera in Central Park

I. The Proper Ladies

The proper ladies
in their folding chairs
will not sit
upon the ground.

They laugh away
the entreaties
of the crowd
to remove themselves:
After all,
you can't _see_ music,
can you?
Silly to think
it will make a difference
when the sun goes down.

II. The Five Chinese Girls

The five
Chinese girls,
who have
three dogs,
sit
in a circle
giggling
into their bowls
of rice.
This makes
the dogs,
who are lying
at the edges
of the blanket,
turn to look
inside the circle.

When it starts
to rain
they put
Chinese newspapers
on their heads
and one covers
a dog
with a plastic bag.
When the opera begins
there are
two Chinese girls
facing the ball park.

III. Boy on a Bicycle

The boy
on a bicycle
rides the audience.
Thin long limbs
keep turning
small circles
of people,
leaving great loops
in the grass.

From one group
to another,
he leans
over the handlebar,
balancing words,
shifting time
from right foot to left.

His audience looks
toward the cellos,
who are now
balancing their bows
for a sweeter music.

IV. Boy on a Trash Can

This edge
is hard

can stretch my legs, though
down on the blankets
they're packed
foot to butt

not me
I'm free

In the Tomb of Pernebi, Metropolitan Museum of Art

Fragment of acacia
partial moon
the broken flight of falcon wings

recumbent ibex
eye of Horus

words made of birds
and waves without crest

lotuses showered by hieroglyphs miss
blossoms as if plucked

They come
the food bearers
the life givers
comfort to kings
distant voices
at the mouth of the tomb
entering by electric light what once was
lit by eye of torch
They come
leading goats on tender leashes
snow-throated geese
in the clutch of slender fingers
Fluted hands offer
cakes and wine
shoulders the weightless sheaves
of papyrus
Through narrow passages
they come
feeling their way
by the flats of their palms

Room after room
we elude false doors
approaching
the burial chamber

sarcophagus--
red stone shaped to the coffin inside
holds the body wrapped
in swaddling clothes
resins and spices
breath on the air

Stone-big sleeping Egyptians
hear this voice calling
hold me
save me a place
in your close and silent tomb

I'll keep you company
lie down in the close of your feet
as you gaze straight up
smiles stripped by grave robbers

Tonight I too will sleep
self-embraced
comfortable at last

my bed
a replica of the one at home

The Circle Line

Whatever our burdens,
we can briefly set them down.
This is diplomatic soil, Pier 83,
that middle ground from which
they cannot claim us.
For 3 hours nothing but a breeze
and the sun's silky light
will bear upon our shoulders.
Loops of gulls will draw our boat
in an easy circle around Manhattan.
Any semblance of adulthood we possessed
is cast away.
We are jumpy as schoolchildren,
tickets damp in the cradles of our palms.

The engines are revving up, and already
the logo of the Circle Line, a rakish sailor's knot,
is doing a jig on the starboard side.
And although this is no ocean voyage--
no steamer trunks or dime novels--
still, those who have boarded
dot the upper deck like confetti
and wave to well-wishers
who will shortly be joining them
to lean over the glossy rail kept smooth
not by the meticulous attention of varnish
but by several coats of bright green paint.

Even before we are free of our moorings,
familiar sights come back to us,
the welcome spur of memory's war horses:
the tip of Battery Park thrown out over the water
like a picnic blanket;
the mighty Brooklyn Bridge against whose neck
the hum of cars is a sweet vibrato;
Ellis Island,
the rude mistress of rejected souls,
now herself rejected,
and wearing the reproach of a forsaken lover.

Soon after Gracie Mansion
most of us turn from the rail
to step inside for hot dogs and popcorn.
Between here and home
there is nothing but ragged river
and islands too small to be mapped
set adrift like poor relations.

If ever these were paved,
they are mostly green now.
Everywhere tufts of grass
have made it through,
and close to shore
moss-covered pilings lean into each other
like giant asparagus.

Dogs who have never known pedigree
sit outside wooden shacks a man could not
stand up in, and follow our progress
the way children do a passing train.
Abandoned wheels like spokeless
in the weeds.
Even the trees look broken,
as if they keep meeting with accidents.
Between the shards of pottery,
wild flowers turn up purple
and red and yellow faces.
A tall, dark-skinned man digging a garden
lifts his head to watch us pass,
his thin, hard body angled against the sky
like a farming implement.
For a moment
he anchors us in the shallows,
then slides his spade
into overturned soil.

Just ahead, a tug is pushing up river
like an old shoe. Strong, tough, witty little boat.
Manhattan glints in its wake,
a pearly set rigged against the heavens.
We are beginning to churn up foam.
By the time we reach the dock,
the mop tied to stern
will be washed by white water.

At the Elgin Cinema

At the Buster Keaton movie,
Uncle Izzy poked us in the back.
He spotted us
from the row behind,
popped up,
clapped our shoulders
into his loose, gray sweater.

Buster Keaton
tottered under fire:
Uncle Izzy shook smiles,
punched us together like an accordion
while Keaton was spinning off
a dizzy round of fists.

Uncle Izzy quaked and quivered:
a kaleidoscope splitting colors
to Keaton's black and white.

Mother and Son, The Cloisters

He is very small,
her son;
she can easily hold him.
She cradles his heavy head
against her breast
and slips an arm beneath
his legs, jackknifed at the knees.
Only his slender feet,
stiffly poised
for a childhood portrait,
and his arms,
caught like a child's flailing out before sleep,
lie outside the compass of her lap.
A scant cloth covers his narrow loins,
and though he gives no sign of being cold,
she begins to wrap him in her abundant robes.

A period of grace: quickly,
before the others return,
she lets her fingers play in his hair,
knowing she cannot wake him from this sleep.
She need not fear
the bruises on his hands
nor the deep cut in his side--these will pass.
How many times has she seen
his cuts and bruises!

No cry breaks
his lips, no word--look at him:
not even an eyelid's fluttering...
yes, yes, he is beautiful, her son.
She will hold him,
and kiss his wounds.

The Nightmare (of the Devoted Manhattanite)

We must leave
everything we love:

> The World Trade Center shot in a pitchy sky,
> and viewed in our living room windows
> spangled with its own tiny stars,
> 3 frames per evening;
> our summer *passegiate* on St. Luke's Place,
> arm in arm beneath the lindens;
> the annual Christmas sing,
> voices of friends lifted above mufflers
> and the scrunch of boots
> on the dense, resonant snowpack--
> *les neiges d'antan* --the snows of all the years--

>> "You know what I mean?"
>> "Are you kiddin' me, Lady?"

> movies from the thirties
> dinner out
> delicatessens
> cabs without shocks
> Central Park

our need for space--

> We are in a large house
> by the sea:
> indoors and outdoors space
> never-ending.
> From diminishing boxes
> we draw out
> our few possessions
> out of context here
> among multiplying rooms.

At evening, alone,
we watch surf break
over the rocks that drop down to the beach
until exhausted,
we sleep.

Our bed is a mattress on the floor.
The boxspring hasn't arrived.
I sink into salt dreams that carry us
away from here
by the road that runs
past the house into town…maybe
Manhattan.

LOVE'S POEMS

Sea Time

Where the ping of salt startles the skin
and the cries of sea horses like discordant cellos
recall the pungent air of birth;
where ridges of sand formed in the suck of currents
string necklaces to the coral
and the shake and shimmer of light slips
like an after-image into the envelope of the sea

there is no greater love we can make
than in this enduring brine.

Fresh from the hulls of ships,
the pale specks of marine life,
you break water with the sightings of whales,
offering me the dark, wet cup of your hand.
Between the smack and slap of the waves,
you take in air, your mouth agape
with mother-of-pearl,
your movements delicate, feminine,
for such a large mammal.
Your eyes are closed, and it looks as if
you are dying, but I know that as
the position in which you swim.
You turn your head to shake out water;
shells drop from your ears.

Oh I am a reluctant swimmer.
I stand at the ocean's lip,
the nibble of fish at my heels.
Over the high pitch of the waves
the witty giggles of dolphins assail me
like the divine madness of love.
Ropes of seaweed gather around my ankles
and pull me toward the swell of the surf.

That we could leave something
of this union, something born
of our breath! You kiss me
in the embrace of the vasty deep;
minnows swim out
and tickle my gums.
Your eyes are lights through the ocean's scrim.
Sea anemones wave at us from their umbilical cords,
their bright heads washed in the blood of the fish.
I try to say "I love you"
but it comes out "Blub blub oooo...."

In a fold of rock, protected by the skins
of stones, we hug and hump
until sleep winds her tentacles around us
and we rest flat as rays.
With each push and pull of the ocean,
our blanket of sand draws ever closer.

Convivium Ostiae

for my sister and me, for our beautiful day together

If it wasn't exactly a banquet,
as the title implies,
there wasn't much of a dining room either.
Nothing of the long tables at which
the diners would have lain,
nor the play of strolling musicians--
the soft clop of sandals on marble.
So we reclined upon the accommodating grass,
propped on one elbow as other guests
before us, and let the singing of birds
be our lute. And since there is no Latin word for
"picnic" as such, and since as we ate
we caught the pungent fragrance of wild grapes,
one could indeed say we enjoyed
a "convivium"--a banquet.

We spread our meal beneath the ancient sky:
fresh, wet cheeses, plum tomatoes,
a loaf of bread, smoked meats,
small, dark olives, and that enduring mineral water
which could well have been drawn
from Ostia's springs.

Who could doubt the grandeur of this house
whose remaining portico lifts
among the umbrella pines
like a monument to forgotten gods.
(A man's home, it seems, was his temple too.)
And then the poignant entrance to--what?
There is little of the hall but sky
and a floor stretching toward the horizon
like a mosaic carpet upon which
one might walk to heaven.
And what colors! Fiery blues,
handsome blacks! And then,
as if someone had wished to inject a softer spirit,
a delicate weave of the palest pink.
Of the atrium there survives only
a headless statue under whose blind watch
most of the brick has long been lifted

by earthquakes and thieves,
leaving a ruin of rooms in the grass.
The rest belongs to crumbling time.

"Over here!" my sister cries,
giving me the high sign from behind
a fragment of plaster still holding
a tint of paint.
She is standing in a bathroom conceived
on a resort scale: long expanses of
white marble invaded by streaks of vermilion,
a choir of vents for a steam room,
and a floor that is a romance of the sea.

She turns to me, sweeping her hand toward the bath
in a grand gesture. Pure pleasure shows beneath
the half-moons of her eyelids,
and she is cast in a classic smile,
the corners of her mouth little ironic tucks.
I consider my own features--the sharp, straight nose,
that particular profile--and for a moment
it seems that we, not this house,
are the legacy of the Romans.
"I can almost hear the splash of water!" she says.

In the market nearby, where surely
the cook picked through the nectarines,
there is not the
flutter of a toga disappearing into a shop.
With our hands we brush away
a veil of pine needles
obscuring the sidewalk:
there the tradesmen's signs--
a shaft of wheat, two fish in swim--
remain like banners long after the parade has passed.
Indeed, everywhere we look
there are signs: Welcome to Ostia,
Festival Today, This Way to the Baths,
Beware of the Dog.

We marvel at this--as if civilized life
were something we invented,
and history merely amateurs bungling the script.

Ostia speaks:
from the crevices in the walls,
from the cracks in the floors,
in the wind, in the branches of the pines,
at every step we take,
muffled cries, giggles, and whispers.
We whirl about: nothing.
But the moment we turn our backs,
more voices at our heels!
I catch my foot, sure it is being held
by invisible hands--but no, it's only
the tug of the sorrel.
Suddenly I see graffiti on a tree:
CASSIUS TERTIAM AMAT
--but no, it's only the pattern of bark in sunlight.

It's late afternoon now,
and we are making our way back
through Ostia's main street,
two cheerful drunks stumbling
in the deep grooves worn by the carts
of the Romans.
The sky has given up its ferocious blue
to a dusting of copper.
We're high, all right,
but Bacchus has nothing to do with it.
It is, quite simply, love:
the past we share, ancient and present,
the runes we have inscribed on one another's hearts.
When I trip again, my sister cries: "That's three!"
Now we are helpless with laughter, the red basket
with the remains of our meal
trembling between us.

We have reached the gates of the city.
Behind us, Ostia lies in the arms of the sunset.
Ahead, the road continues, distinguished now

not by houses and shops but graves,
the first thing you see coming in,
and the last thing you see going out.
Markers set to the ground
as firmly as a farewell kiss, and bearing still
the names of the dead:
Beloved Flavius, Tender Messalina.
Built for posterity, yes.
But acknowledging death, also yes.
Why else so close to home, a mere step
between those committed to earth,
and those who have not yet reached
the cooling stones.

for Eddie...and for my former husband

Eddie asks me,
When is the torture over?
and as I cross the room to touch his shoulder,
the floor dogs me like a Greek chorus saying,
Remember, remember, remember...
I too was once at the break of marriage,
and even now
memory releases her quarry.

He weeps at my kitchen counter,
its backdrop of tiles the vivid blues and golds
of Seville.
I remember a shop whose floor is powdered
with the cool stone dust of foundries
and the filtery light of cathedrals.
My husband and I are buying tiles for the kitchen
by holding up fingers to say
how many.
The shopkeeper nods attentively
and as he does
I notice that he too is powdered
with a fine, light dust.
Later, at home, unpacking tiles,
we discover one which has been struck without an S
and says
MADE IN PAIN.

Eddie,
once I too dreaded dusk, the nights banked with pillows
to shore up darkness.
Dug into sheets, I kept the forest from my bed
only to be pulled from dreams by distant howling- -
my own crying.
But there are days now
when I never think of him,
as if he's slipped out of my life unnoticed,
leaving the clutter of love
to be packed and stored for the clean sweep
of daily living.
And when I remember what I've forgotten,

I tie a string around my heart
so I won't forget
what I know I can.

And if at evening Eddie asks me,
When is the torture over?
I touch his shoulder
that he might cry
a while.
How can I tell him,
Never.

and those roses!

I.

You have chosen a restaurant
reminiscent of Key West:
a broad, white cafe open to the world
on one side only;
long, dark wood tables
as if for a Brueghel wedding,
but set with cutlery so that
everyone faces the street.
A few have turned sideways
toward their companions, or have
draped themselves over unoccupied chairs
in the languorous positions of
acrobats at rest.

The tables have been sanded to silk:
plates make soft thuds
when set down.
Everywhere carafes of wine are
catching the light--rubies here, topazes there--
liquid never quite still but
moving ever so slightly, slipping
up and down the glass.
There are bird cries very close
and the air seems fragrant
although there are no flowers in sight.

II.

Those roses you gave me
are blooming on my piano
like twelve scarlet fires.
As if that four-hour lunch
in the open-air whitewash of the sun
were not enough.

You wore an open shirt
and there was that delicious pie wedge
of your chest
covered with soft, dark hair.
Equally irresistible are those full
half-moons of your mouth,
making you look perpetually hungry.

Later, we are sitting side by side in the car
with that long distance across the seat.
You have your glasses on and are
concentrating on the road.
Suddenly you pull over,
dip into the back seat
like a magician into a hat,
and draw out a bouquet of
red, red roses,
a final gesture which really overwhelms me.
As you pull back into traffic,
I ask you what it's like to be a young lawyer
then watch your mouth move
to form words.
I am filled with the fragrance of roses
and the distance between us seems to be closing
although we are still in our places.
I am dreaming about slipping my hand
along the back of the seat
till my fingers reach the nape of your neck,
but the moment, I know, is complete:
I have enough to take home--
all that sun, that shirt, that mouth,
and those roses!

Sailing at Sheepshead Bay

The sea is choppy today,
the result of recent storms.
You sit to stern, the tiller in your hand,
while I, at the bow, watch for
oncoming craft and whitecaps.
The string at the top of the jib is tangled
so we cannot tell wind direction except by
the set of the sail.

The beginnings of light--pink and peach--shoot down
from the cloudy sky like fingers
pointing toward the water.
A bright orange sunfish drops out of the horizon
and makes its way along the Manhattan skyline.
I see you speak but mostly the wind
catches your words and blows them away.

This trip has been difficult for me.
I'm all off kilter from the ups and downs.
You, I know, could stay here longer,
going it alone in uncertain water.

We are starting home,
hitting the swells
in our borrowed boat.
The sail seems willing
and goes suddenly full.
We are hoping for buoys
as we reach warmer water.
Meantime, we pull together,
keeping the dock in mind.

Margie

Margie didn't have her teeth till last year, and oh!
was she happy when she got them!
Sparks returned to her eyes like children
coming in from play.
The rouged hollows of her cheeks, once a parody
of youth, now tender a blush of smiles. Smiles cause
the bright red of her lipstick to seep into
ravines around her mouth, each delicate wrinkle
following a course upward, tracing the rolling hills
of her native Ireland.

When she sees my husband and me, she says,
"Look at him! He's so beooteeful, darlin'!
And you! So pretty!
At first I thought you didn't like me--stupid old Margie--
you passed me in the street
and never said a word.
Now I know better. The way that I need my teeth, darlin',
you need yer glasses!

"And how's yer little daggie,
yer sweet little daggie?
Home, is he?
And what a lovely home he has!

"Sometimes I get so lonely, darlin's,
I have my little nieces over, darlin' little girls.
But I'm so old, you know, and they pull the cat's tail,
and one time he ran away and I was two days
gettin' him back!

"And how's yer little daggie,
yer sweet little daggie?

"You know, darlin's both, my life has been hard--
not a moment's peace, God knows,
from back home to here.
But they gave me a job at the church,
servin' coffee after mass Sunday mornin's, isn't it lovely?
And if I'm late, they all say, 'Where's Margie?'

"And how's yer little daggie,
yer sweet little daggie?

"You be good to each other now.
The two of you! So beooteeful! Perfect
just the way you are!
You know, darlin',
when I first met your husband,
I was so unhappy!
Then I met him, and my life changed!
He smiled so, and talked to me, darlin'.
He said, 'Margie, get yer teeth
and you'll see what a difference'!
I thought God had come, I did, darlin'.
I told Father Flannigan that God
had come to me, and he said, 'Margie,
'tisn't God, but a good young man
who loves you.'"

Velvet Pants
    to a friend

You say you think of me
in the most innocent ways,
defining ''affair'' by consummation.
And though I would have thought of it rather
as something which obsesses,
like a song you can't stop singing,
still, we agree on one point:
this is no *poème d'amour,*
so let's be friends.
I'll settle for you in public places--
restaurants and the like--
as long as you keep from the waist down
under the table.
You see, my dear, I can withstand your alluring habits--
that way you have of softly smacking the corners of your mouth
to punctuate sentences,
that run your tongue does between your lips.
But once I see those velvet pants
there's nothing but the Lord can save me:
I cease to focus on what you say, find myself imagining instead
the look and feel of your sex
were I caught in the vise of those velvet thighs.

You tell me you're looking for someone to love, that
you're not in love with anyone now.
I offer to introduce you to a friend,
but you say, ''No more. Let's not talk about her.''
''She's very fuckable, this friend of mine,'' I say.
(How civilized, how open-mined I am.)
''That's just what I think about you,'' you reply,
moving a leg into the open
as you tell me you've watched my breasts move inside my blouses
and wonder what the nipples look like, taste like, in the flesh.

One evening, as you're walking me home after dinner,
we pass a gallery showing sculptures--
women's upper torsos in plaster of Paris--
and you remark on the squishy yet erect state of the nipples:
''Done while they were lying down--obvious''
to which I reply, ''You can leave me here. We're close enough.''
''How close are we?'' you say, angling your mouth,

hot as always, toward mine.
"Very cl--" but you cut me off, movie-style,
sealing her mouth with a kiss,
only mine is open, waiting for you.
"That was lovely," you say, "delicious the way your hand
rested against my crotch as we kissed."
I would like to slip my hand beneath the sea-green surface of your velvet pants, dipping into salty brine
to bring up sea stones.

(In a dream I had
I was lying in a vast bath, my back and head resting against
the slurpy sides of the tub.
You emerge from the water, slide your slick slim body over mine:
your mouth, persistent but patient, tastes of salt,
your tongue a sea anemone looking for a place to sting.)

You want to know if I can be with you
and do without?
Which Me are you asking?

When we've said our goodnights, and
turned our backs to pace off,
reluctant duelers,
I turn early to watch you walking away,
your ass velveted in moonlight.

They say the way to rid yourself
of a persistent tune is to sing it through,
beginning to end, once for all,

and so I'm singing, my love,
all your interminable verses...

Scorpio's Fire
> *for Ree Dragonette*

You were a storm of Scorpio fire,
Florentine eyes in spontaneous combustion.
The dynamo power of your slight frame
bent stars to your hand,
pulled the very planets from their places,
and put them back.
The moon shone full for you.

To hear your poems was to be moved geomorphically,
    astrologically.
You were scientist: alchemist and astronomer,
observer of stars, the makeup of quartz, bound
to the human heart, the poet in you.
I trusted your complex of geological strata,
your rainbow spectrum, that wish
to touch your thigh to a lover's.

If I could write a paean to you, Ree, I would engage the heavens in
    my aid,
the night, the wind, the fire to my grasp.
But I am not a wielder of heavenly things.
No stars or planets make their home in me.
I am a poet of simpler occasions--
dog at the corner,
day at the beach.
And so I give you

foxglove, say,
or moonstone.

for Lucio

Each year,
blood eluded you.
It was always just beyond
your reach, a fine silk
that slipped your fingers.
And then, at sixteen,
you lay in a hospital bed,
your only hope transfusion,
that well-intentioned gift
like a suit that never quite fits.

Struck from birth with a fatal anemia,
you were born into this world
lacking blood and breath,
pale, dying,
even as they took you
from the womb.
No period of grace for you,
no forty years before the pallor sets in,
the bones begin to crack.

"Thalassemia," from the Greek *thalassa,*
as if your deadly affliction
were linked to the sea.

Toward the end, you could not be alone,
and who could blame you?
Week after week, your brother
sat by your bedside, reading to you,
bringing news of the village,
holding your hand
as dark came on, each day
a little part of him
dying with you.

Your brother, night after sleepless night,
the shallows under his eyes deeper and deeper,
your brother who cried in the few hours
when you slept, not wishing
to burden you further, forcing food
down his own unwilling throat so that you
might share a meal.

Lucio, too weak, finally, even to eat,
but strong enough to face your own death,
to raise your colors
before letting go that tenuous thread.

Your last wish was to be carried
to the beach, that shore above which
your town has perched for 2,000 years.
You wanted to see the tide once more,
feel the breeze off the waves,
watch gulls picking among the ruins of
Tiberius's villa, about which your brother said:
"Well, what's the difference? It's been here
2,000 years. It'll be here 2,000 more."

I remember that beach:
how the white-washed town sits on a cliff
that drops to the sand, a sight
tourists would pay dearly to see,
except that, *grazie a dio,* they haven't discovered
Sperlonga, whose very name is a wish,
a longing, a hope.

And so, Lucio, I think of you
as I sit on a beach in New York,
nothing like the spectacular, heart-breaking shore
at Sperlonga. But still,
the tide is the tide,
and as I look at gulls picking among
abandoned sand castles, and,
as it happens,
listening to a singer
who bears your name,
I watch your soul floating above the water,
embraced by the wind,
buoyed up, finally,
by the sea.

To a Friend Who Shakes in the Morning

I find your morning shakes delightful,
as if coming into the day
makes you tremble like a baby.
I watch you leave the bed with trepidation
and tenderly approach the kitchen,
hands quickening
to turn up the gas.

You explain this as a temporary paralysis,
some benign brain damage which releases its grip
as the sun fully ascends and lights the world.

I find these explanations doubtful,
given the limited nature of the impairment
and the considerable extent of your talents,
but I'm in no mood to argue:
I'm listening to the kettle being dragged
to its burner,
for the mute crash of cups
against the sink.

Yes, it's very sweet how you approach
each day shaking.

Poem for Miles Davis

*"Didn't your mama ever tell you that hanging out with Negroes
and listening to jazz music ain't gonna bring you no good?"*
                                                --a friend

Used to be I couldn't sleep at night,
could not keep worry from my mind.
But I found the cure for bad dreams
when I discovered sweet cream
at my door...

In the welcome hands of midnight,
I turn on a tape
when I turn out the light.
I spread like butter beneath the sheet...

I got Miles to go
before I sleep.

Oh Creator of star-touched sky lines,
more facile than a lover's rime,
I'm strung in the plexus of 4/4 time,
your dawn...

Make me your melody,
your note to be slid upon, hit upon.
Encourage me with variations--anticipation--
blow sweet nothings in my ear...

When you're close,
I hear "Funny Valentine,"
I taste those full-blown lips swallow mine,
then you're gone...

I'm expecting resolution,
but you hit a blue one:
you're on the ceiling--revolution!

I got to jump up
from the bed,
reach as high as I can

I feel your hand:
the light engage of fingertips
then you rip

pulling me
trip and stumble
thru the percussion,
over the bass,
we leap the sax

down dark, wet streets
lit by the dusky sparkle
of your horn

We're starting toward rooftops
bound for galaxies

We're up
and we never hit ground.

When the vibes come in,
we're gone...

miles and miles and miles away...

We hit home with moon rocks,
the fiery streak of meteors:
the bed is alive with syncopation--anticipation--
that triple tonguing up and down my spine,
no more bad dreams
only sweet cream...

Come blow your horn
between my thighs--
I'm under your starlit tune, Miles,
but you must come soon, Miles!

After the Death of My Shoemaker

Where will I take my shoes
now?
I've let a pair run down to nails
without you.
Every once in a while
I think about taking them to your old shop
but I never do. I find myself
walking on the other side of Bleecker Street,
avoiding the storefront where
so often I stopped
to talk,
to watch you working at the wheel. Shoes
were my calling card.

At Christmastime,
when the boots in your shop were piled high as
the snow outside,
you cleared a space for me.
Little crowds passed on Bleecker Street,
walking against the cold.
You brushed bits of leather
from your apron, gave me a cup of wine.
We toasted the season.

Shall I keep my run-down heels
to remember you by?

FOUR DOGS AND A SHEEP

For John Dog

You never heard
of poems

they're not like
sit or
down or
stay

not like
anything you know.

So while
you were
poised there
quiet
in a rare
moment

I thought
I'd give you
your first

in exchange
for the times
you kept
my feet warm
last winter.

Dog Days

Where does he go
when I'm not here?

Is the wicker chair
the seat of
his morning fantasies?
Where are those corners
I never see?
Corners in which he keeps his stash
of bones and rags?

Where does the sun fall
at 4:00?
Is he there?
In that circle
of light?

Window Box

It was summer, our new apartment.
The orange hassock--a color I detest--
had been pushed up to a window sill
and abandoned like an overgrown squash.

We had bought that hassock
so that he--our dog--could have
a view of the street from six stories up.
We had spent weeks looking for it--
the right size, the right shape, large enough,
soft enough, hard enough (the color
was always wrong)
and then weeks waiting for him to use it.

Not that he did so.
Oh no.
His disinterest was profound.
This hassock did not exist.
We coaxed, we bribed,
we patted the orange surface lovingly.
We even went so far as to kneel on the thing
and stick our faces out the window,
feigning extravagant interest in the street.

At last he sighed, got up,
and edged toward the hassock as if
we were door-to-door salesmen whose product
he felt obligated to try.
We watched the inspection:
the circling, the sniffing, the pawing, the licking,
and, finally, dismissal.
"It's real leather!" I cried.

Then one day his decision broke.
For no apparent reason,
he roused himself from slumber,
ambled toward the hassock--
already slightly faded--
and stepped up as gingerly
as a king upon a throne.
He placed his paws on the sill

and stuck his nose through the geraniums
and petunias.
The screen was open.

Ah, the pleasure of discovery!
Indifference slips like a mask
from a smile. He has glimpsed not only
the street but indeed the heavens:
a man sunbathing on a roof on West Fourth Street,
the steeple of the Seventh Day Adventist Church,
birds, planes, chimneys, skylights, smoke stacks,
now his turf, his domain.

I can see him still:
the long, arched line of his back
as he leans forward to greet the realm,
tail straight out like a banner,
ears pricked for heartbeats,
the fur starting from his spine
like small ideas.

William Steig's Dogs

William Steig's dogs
never get what they want.

This one,
clinging to the edge
of the buffet table,
claws a thin line
at the human banquet,
a spread of cakes at bay
he can't
        quite
            grab.

Sheep

At the Bank Street Fair:
the sheep
oval as blimps,
bigger than dogs.

On four stiff legs
they wait.

I put my hand
into the
thick, springy stuff
of sheep:
a thousand rugs
beneath my fingers.

ANIMA/ANIMUS

Anima

I never do what I'm told.
I never do what I'm asked.
If I have a notion, I take it.
I do what I want.
As Goddess of the Weak,
the Forgotten, the Mute,
I am unruled paper--that innocent field
on which I battle elements more unprincipled
than I.
That's what comes of not being born, like Athena,
full-blown from the head of Zeus.
How else could I take in strays,
direct the lost, provide the dying
with coins?

I used to play by the rules.
When the rug was pulled,
when the floor collapsed,
I went down crying out
for sanity and justice,
reason and good nature.
But I got smart.
Now when I feel the floor give way,
I drop with good grace
and kiss the hand that lets the trap.
I play dead:
then I mount the shoulders of my would-be hangman,
transcending crossbeams
and the limbs of the dead.
Who better prepared
than herself denied?

In matters of defense, my advice is:
Never defend yourself.
Be nice to those who hate you.
Be calm with the furious.
Smile when everyone else is crying.
Weep during comedies.
In other words, screw them.
And never let them know
what you really think.
Let the hangmen hang themselves.
Believe me, there'll be rope enough.

If I Were This Box, What Would I Hold?
for Charles

Stepping into someone else's shoes
is not so much a question of fit
as taking the ground anew.
Not so much, What do I look like?
as, What pulse does the ground give
when I walk in other shoes?
Where the rains are quick and light,
if I were a leaf,
it would not be so much a question of
the makeup of fibers, as knowing that
for such rains I must be a deep, green bowl,
a wellspring for water.

It's not so much observation as knowing
that part of you which is a part
of all else: If I were this pen,
what would I write, If I were this dial,
what would I tell? and so on.
Not so much, under the microscope,
as me under it,
recognizing in that hug of cells
my very own face.

It's less taking apart
than putting together, less looking on
that jumping in,
for who can recall the elements of mud?
But if you were a frog, you would willingly slip
beneath that tepid blanket,
for you know very well what mud is.

It's not so much a question of
seeking as remembering.
It's like mental free rein:
Don't be so sure the horse
doesn't know the way home.
From one path, he knows many.
And though he may never have trod here,
nor know the components of mud,
yet his hooves feel the sodden earth,
the grit of soil, as if they were his own.
Which of course they are.

In the dark of night,
no fear will be dispelled
by the use of your eyes,
nor the notion that boogie-men do not exist.
Because of course they do.
But remember, then, that it is not so much
a question of thinking as holding:

Now close your eyes,
and feel the room come up to your feet.
There's your bedside lamp,
its light, like yours, extinguished
for sleep.
The corners of your room
hold nothing you do not know.
Bear in mind
the niches in your heart,
those shadow places,
as they meet
their very own darkness.

The Vegetable Garden at Kent Cliffs, New York

In orderly rows
the cabbages sit down.
Immense lavender fans spread wide,
they flap at the summer breeze,
great stupid matrons
cooling their closed, hard hearts,
still duchesses
though small insects eat holes
in their outer leaves.

Monsters

We see them as cumbrous, hulking,
good hearts trapped
by unwieldy matter,
not really meaning to
disturb houses or rip trees
from our careful lawns.

We forgive them their green skin,
the bat wings folded
beneath their shirts,
their long teeth and wolf faces,
as they stumble toward us
vying for love.

We've created them unaware
of their own transformations,
those sudden changes brought on by
a delicate white neck or
a child picking flowers in an open glen.
We watch when,
overcome by forces--emotions--we ourselves
cannot explain,
they run amok in our cities,
pulling whole buildings into their graceless paths
as they seek some one who can
understand their blundering hearts.

We know,
we've been there
on those flood-lighted nights when,
turned to dogs,
we find ourselves crazed
under the moon

Moonstone Beach, Rhode Island

Above the rocks
that drop
to the beach:
Victorian mansions
in the cold stone sky.

Against the iron dawn
parapets rise,
might fly banners.

White verandahs
flounce their lacy skirts
onto the stiff, dark grass.

Beads
pinnacles
finials
tracery
fringes
filagree
defy straight lines,
will not be made to mind.

To a Monk Who Finds His Teacher in Bed with His Best Friend

Just as spring is returning to the west,
you return from the east,
ordination crisp as a daffodil,
to find your teacher, a monk too,
in bed with your best friend.
The waters of India are long behind you--no chance
of a healing dip in the Ganges
to cure the creep of reality
across your skin.

Monked or not,
the world is the world,
dear friend.
There really are no sacred cows.
Desire can't be cloaked by
the red robes of the order: the altar serves
many a spiritual transvestite--garb is not necessarily
cause for trust.

Despite this prick in your faith,
karma would have it that
every one is a teacher,
and every thing a lesson, even this monk
in your bed: look how quickly he's lifted the weight
of illusion, those burdensome dictates about monks--
and "friends."

Just watch out for the pretty boys, and *especially* the holy,
those rigid folk who make the rules that are made
to be broken, all to hide their discomfort
at the touch of spring.
Do not follow them--they are not leaders
but vanity's yes-men, easily herded
by the most common calls.
Beware of sheep in monk's clothing.

Switzerland

they just started
taking it down,
that's all

all of a sudden
someone was
shouting orders

and they struck
the set

the cardboard backdrop
was collapsed
like a folding screen

and ten thousand
neatly terraced fields
came face to face
with the Matterhorn

it was too late
at that point
to tell someone
it was all a mistake

that the edelweiss
which bloomed wax-like
on _that_ hillside was real

by that time,
four men
were already
trying to balance
Geneva on one end
and a herd of cows
on the other

From a Pompeian Wall Painting

Lady,
you pluck that flower
as if you've done it before:
you pick with such delicate tension,
snipping the pale stem
between thumb and forefinger.

Or could it be
that you are Spring itself?
That those slender fingers
have not plucked, but,
drawing a flower from your cornucopia,
fix its green stem
onto Winter's stubble.

Karl Wallenda: 1905-1978
--San Juan, March 22

Death was otherwise,
he believed. The earth was merely
a place to set your rigging.
To live was to walk the wire, to span
circuses, streets, cities, continents--
and all without a net.
It tempts a fall,
he said.

So when he fell,
nothing could stop him

He fell,
still clutching his balancing stick,
still holding something
representing the wire

3 seconds:
a long time to go down
watching the ground come up

He fell,
coming down hard on the cab,
bouncing to the street
like a marionette
whose strings have been cut,
the body less a body
than a dummy pitched earthward
to replace him,
to simulate death.

Mr. Wallenda lies in the street, his balancing stick at his feet.

The announcer's voice--
tight whispered words balanced on his vocal cords,
the tension on the wire

The announcer's voice- -
swayed by a gust of wind
stronger than the rest,
wavering as Wallenda wavers upon the wire

The announcer's voice- -
slipping midway
as Wallenda loses footing but still grips
his balancing pole, its wings trembling

The announcer's voice- -
out of control,
plunging to the street
in breaking Spanish- -

A wind. Only a wind. Many times before
I have walked in a wind like that.

In Detroit
a slip of the foot left him swaying
at the edge of the void,
preserved only by balance and courage

and still the whole pyramid came apart in mid-air:

Wallendas clinging to the wire,
Wallendas plunging to the floor.

And now it's a gust of wind
that vibrates the cable.

Ich kann nich mehr halten- -I can't hold on any longer!

Sit, Poppy, sit!

Wallenda crouches. The wind
jars him.

At the hospital
he is pronounced dead:
massive internal injuries.

To fall and keep falling,
nothing to interrupt your descent,
to fall in a nightmare helpless,
waking startled, stomach turning,
the dream having faded,
blotted out by the terror of falling,
of losing your grip at curbside,
or a flight of steps,
but for Wallenda it's
no dream
no net

He wears red ballet slippers,
the seam on the inside,
creating a smooth surface
on which to walk.

Patriarch,
wire dancing beneath you,
and beneath you
the most famous troupe of high-wire walkers
in circus history
watch their father lose his balance: a cable
strung between beachfront hotels.

I feel better up here
than I do down there. Down there
I break all to pieces...

...blown off the wire,
Karl Wallenda, dead,
at 73.

The Night Train to St. Louis

I.

On the night train
to St. Louis
the tumbling
has stopped.
The jugglers
are asleep,
their bowlers and oranges
in the aisles.

The gymnast,
head down,
knees hard
to his chest,
is preparing for
a double somersault,
and the aerialist
grips the seat back,
barely catches
a footrest.

II.

The Amish couple
sleep under squares
of different colors.

Their afghan
neat farms.

French knots
are silos.

Along the borders
horse-drawn carts
trot in running stitches.

The Amish couple
dream in pastures:
yellow and green counterpane,
their countypane.

When My Sister Plays the Cello
for Valeria

When my sister
plays the cello
its muscular body
springs
like the red-round
buttocks
of a horse
jumping a fence
catching the sun
in its polished coat.

She bends to the fingerboard
a horse's neck
stretched
and grazing
her cheek.

When she
plays the cello
her fingers touch
the red-brown
of its wooden coat

hit the top note
pluck
the strings of
horse throats
and the cello
whinnies.

Butcher-Hands Fantasy

the butcher's hands
are big, red, wide
chewed

the butcher's hands
will be thrown
to the customers
at feeding time

while cutting chops
the butcher
lines up the cleaver
alongside his hand
and

cuts off the hand
instead

he weighs it
wraps it up
and says $2.89 please

SPECIAL TODAY:
Butcher Hands

Animus, Starving Spirit
for Lucille

Animus, starving spirit,
if you hear us, cry out
from the fallen shaft,
from the depths of your mine.
The rubble here is thick:
we tap the surface rock, the collapse
of beams, hoping you still have voice.
We carry our hearts like weights in our chests
but like all who would live
we believe you yet have breath.

Beneath the fallen rock
earth covers me.
I hear them struggling above
yet can tell their location no more
than they mine.
Held in,
denied breath,
I resist a deliverance
that would produce me stillborn.
I take in dust,
bite grit between my teeth.
Do I breathe to reward their labor?
Or do I wish to survive?

One sound can clear the dust--make it.
The seismic rumble is at your heels:
Let the explosions in your feet
thunder through your gut,
roar into your throat--don't stop
till your mouth opens.
Our ears are pressed to the pulse of rock:
Should one cry let go,
we will hear it.

I heard the explosion
but I couldn't speak.
I felt the mine give way
but I couldn't move.
Others were crawling upward
while they could still reach sunlight.
I saw their hands: outstretched beams in the darkness
but I couldn't answer.
The shaft fell in:
I lay there shut of light
in a bed of rock.
I hear my ears filling with earth.
Coal dusts my lips
and comes for my throat.
I open my mouth
and spit cries.

Claudia Menza   *Photo by Bert Andrews*